Alien Prince

Danielle Jacks

Copyright © 2023 Danielle Jacks All rights reserved

Alien Prince © 2023 Danielle Jacks

This book is the work of fiction. Any names, characters, places, and events are either creations of the author's imagination or used fictitiously. Any similarities are purely coincidental.
Copyright © 2023 by Danielle Jacks.
All rights are reserved. Published in the United Kingdom by Danielle Jacks.
No part of this book may be used or reproduced without the author's written consent, except in the case of a brief quotation to enhance reviews or articles.

Editor: Karen Sanders
Cover designer: Danielle Jacks

ALIEN PRINCE BY DANIELLE JACKS

Fate can change a life in a split second.
Naomi New York City is my new home, and I'm hoping to find my first teaching job here. However, when a meteorite threatens to destroy Earth, we need a miracle. Our call is answered by an alien ship. I'm offered my dream job, but there's a catch. The school has agreed to show the alien prince Zenith around the city, and I'm picked to be his guide. Can I impress the school by welcoming our alien guests or will one alien in particular have me thinking of a future in a different location? Zenith Earth is my destination, and I'm hoping to find my mate. When given the choice to save the human planet from the disaster, I must decide if it's worth risking my spaceship.
Naomi is the beautiful woman assigned to show me around New York City. Instantly, I know she's the female for me. Can I convince my mate she's perfect for me, or will I leave Earth with a broken heart?

CHAPTER ONE

Naomi

Brown isn't usually a color I would wear. The matching suit jacket and skirt have a vintage feel that can only be achieved with suede. Striking a pose, I stare at myself in the full-length mirror. I've already tried on half my wardrobe, but I'm desperate for my job interview to go well.

"What do you think?" I ask my best friend and roommate, Sonya.

"You look like a librarian," she says, screwing up her face.

"I'm trying to give them the impression I'm a professional, smart teacher. A librarian should be a compliment, but it isn't when you say it with such distaste." I pout.

"High school teachers are supposed to be hot or old. You've combined the two and you're going to confuse all the teenage boys."

I laugh and roll my eyes. "You have an obscure view of what happens at school." We both know she's only talking about unattainable puppy love, but it's not something I want to encourage. I'd rather be seen as unattractive.

"Don't tell me you didn't have a crush on one single staff member when you were a kid." She crosses her arms like she doesn't believe it's possible.

"You know I'm picky. I only had eyes for the quarterback, and he didn't see me as more than a homework ticket." I shrug. Looking back, the class nerd would never have won the heart of the school rebel.

"It would take someone from another planet to rock your world."

Playfully, I swat her arm. "Anyone would think you got out of bed on the wrong side."

I could find love if I was looking. School is not the place for me to find it. Not in the past and not now. I'd never date a colleague because business and pleasure don't mix. School is about focusing on my career.

"Sorry. I don't mean to sound harsh. You know I love your nerdiness. I'm going to offer a little advice, though. I think you should at least ditch the jacket." I slip it off and re-examine my outfit in the mirror. Sonya stands behind me and wraps her arms around me. "Don't be nervous. You're going to kill this interview."

"Thanks."

I finish getting ready by adding a little makeup and a simple teardrop necklace. The mascara and natural eyeshadow enhance the dark brown of my irises. Once I put my glasses back on, my look is complete. Let's hope it's smart enough to impress.

The sky darkens as I look out of my New York apartment window. I miss the blue sky of the Florida Keys, but if I want to work at one of America's elite schools, I need to prove I can leave the comfort of my hometown. I'm a newly qualified teacher and I'm ready to get my first job in the city.

My phone chimes with a message from my dad. **Good luck.**

I smile. I'm close to my dad. It's been just the two of us since my mom left when I was six. He was the one who had convinced me I needed to fulfill my dream, even though it meant us being separated.

Thank you. I text back.

My dad's wishes are important to me because he's always been my cheerleader. I'm glad he remembered to message me because I needed the extra boost.

Pumps are the only shoe option for a fifth-floor walk-up apartment, and once I'm ready, I head for the stairs. I hope it doesn't rain before I get to my interview.

"Good luck," Sonya shouts as I start to descend the stairs.

"See you soon."

My stomach is doing somersaults as my feet hit the pavement. I make my way down the street towards the subway. A large spot of rain splashes next to my shoe just as I turn the corner. I race to reach cover, but it's too late. I should have brought my coat. Quickly, I make my way onto the train and sit on an empty seat near the back.

Using my camera, I look at myself on the screen. My light brown hair has flattened to my head, but the makeup I applied has stayed in place. Let's hope a bit of water doesn't put them off. I'm usually a forward planner. Today, my nerves are shot, and it's affecting my cognitive function.

The subway wastes no time, and I make it to the interview as the rain starts to ease up. One last glance in my makeshift mirror and I'm sitting in the principal's office. Mrs. Lionel smiles sweetly before taking her seat behind her large oak desk.

"Ms. Allen, it's a pleasure to finally meet you." She ruffles a few papers on her desk, which I'm guessing have the interview questions on.

I moved to New York about a month ago, and I've been pestering her office ever since I arrived. Actually, I've been sending out letters of interest along with my credentials to all the local high schools. Greenview High is the first to offer me a chance of getting a position in their drama department. I'd love to work in one of the top performing arts schools, but first I have to get my foot in the door somewhere.

"It's great to be here," I say, leaning forward to offer my hand, which she gracefully takes. We hold eye contact for a few seconds, and I make sure my grip is firm just like my self-help book, *Great impressions* taught me. The wet sleeve of my top sits awkwardly on my elbow as I pull my arm back, but I try not to fidget.

"How are you adjusting to the city?"

"I miss the sun and beach. Although having food, bookstores, and fast travel at your fingertips is a perk." I laugh nervously.

"I'm glad you're converting to city life." Her smile is tight this time and my stomach jolts. I should've said I hated the beach and the midnight sirens are so much more relaxing. She goes on to ask me the questions written out in front of her while filling in the paperwork. She covers my qualifications, experience, and interests. As interviews go, this one's fairly standard, and I start to relax.

"This will be my first job since qualifying as a teacher, but I completed my work experience and graduated high in my class. I hope you'll strongly consider me as an applicant."

She stands, signaling our meeting is over. Her smile

is warming, yet she gives nothing away. I get to my feet and the water in my pumps squelches.

"Thank you for coming. We'll be in touch."

"Thanks." We shake hands again before I make a swift exit.

The next candidate is sitting outside the office, and I give a faint smile. Only time will tell if they will choose me.

The rain has subsided when I get outside, although there's a trickle of water running along the road. Like most buildings in New York, the school is at the curbside.

I'd arranged a coffee shop meeting with my roommate after the interview, but I text her to say I'd rather go home. I got myself so worked up for the interview I feel drained. She sends me a picture of herself with a group of friends.

I met Sonya on placement last summer. She was visiting Florida for spring break, and I was photographing marine life for the new term. We clicked straight away, and the rest is history. When I said I wanted to move to New York, she practically snapped my hand off for the opportunity to be my roommate. Before we got our walk-up apartment, she was living in Brooklyn with her parents. Together, we both got what we wanted. A space in the city.

I get the subway home and take a shower to clean up from the rain. Once I've freshened up, I put on my lounge suit and sit by the window with my latest book. Scattered rubbish blows past my window and it appears a storm is about to blow in. High-rise buildings create a vortex for the sound of the wind, and the howl is intimidating. Along with the traffic, the noise is difficult to block out. I'm almost two chapters into my contemporary romance before the hustle and bustle of the city fades out and I get my escape.

When I look up from the page, the light from the window is fading at an unnatural rate and people are gathering in front of their homes. Putting down the book, I step outside onto the stairwell to take a closer look. The storm has settled and it's deadly quiet. People everywhere are staring up into the sky with their mouths hanging open. I pull out my phone as my attention is drawn up. The sun is blocked out by a large dark circle in the sky. Unlocking my phone, I pull up my dad's number and press dial. He answers on the second ring.

"Are you seeing this?" I ask without a greeting. An

unsettling feeling churns in my stomach.

"I was about to call you. I've just got off the phone with my old work colleague, Martin. A large meteorite is on its way to Earth, and we don't have the resources to stop it."

"What does that mean? What should we do?" My pulse beats loudly in my ears as I begin to feel light-headed.

"There's nothing we can do. There won't be enough time for us to be together, and if Martin's prediction is correct, the impact could wipe out half the world."

The rock doesn't look that big at the moment, and that's probably an indication of how far away it is. I have no doubt he knows what he's talking about even though it isn't his area of expertise. My career is long forgotten when I realize I might never see my dad again.

CHAPTER TWO

Zenith

"Prince Zenith, we have a problem," Captain Jinker says.

I put down my intergalactic game and look up to find the captain standing to attention. The journey from our home planet, Kamath, which is two galaxies over, has been tiring, even while traveling at light speed.

"What is it?" I ask, hoping it's not something trivial like when we ran out of space noodles again. My men's concept of urgent is lacking in judgment, and honestly, I'll be glad when this trip is over.

"The planet you were going to look for your mate on is about to be hit by a large meteorite."

I almost fall out of my chair as I struggle to my feet. We've traveled all this way. I can't lose my chance at finding a mate when we've specifically chosen this planet for its compatibility. Our species is all male, and the only way I'll carry on the royal bloodline is by finding a suitable female.

"How much damage do you think it will cause?" My father is the reason I'm searching for a mate, and if I come back empty-handed, I'll be forced into another long mission. The plan is to find a woman who is impressed by my pedigree, striking blue skin, and charm, then I will sweep her off her feet so I can return home. I'll offer her a place at my side in the kingdom and all the jewels she can imagine. I haven't met many women, but I'm sure it can't be that hard to find a compatible one.

"It could crush over a third of the life forms on Earth."

"And what do you suggest we do?" There will be two-thirds of the population left. I only want one female. I rub my chin, wondering what would be the best thing for us to do.

"Humans are very sensitive creatures, sir. I think we should intervene and save the planet. The problem is, after we've used that much power, we'll have no choice but to stay on Earth while we charge the ship's battery. Also, our landing might be a little bumpy."

If I choose to be the hero, I'll be stuck on Earth for who knows how long, but if I don't, my bride might be upset about her planet. I'd really like to go home, but not with a fragile female.

My conscience gets the better of me. I can't let people die if I can prevent it. "Give the order that it's going to be a rocky landing."

"Yes, sir." He salutes me before disappearing back to the ship's bridge.

I prepare my quarters for an emergency landing before following him. Everyone's on full alert as I enter the control room. The turbulence starts and I grip the rail in front of the large monitors.

"The meteorite is too big. We need more power. Switch off all unessential appliances," Captain Jinker says.

The lights go out and we're plunged into darkness. Our red laser cuts through the rock while burning gases illuminate the screen.

"How much time do we have before the meteorite

hits the Earth's atmosphere?" I ask. My grip tightens on the rail as pain shoots up my arm. A moment ago, I was wondering if this was a good idea, but now it's a reality, I don't want anyone to die.

"Not enough." Earth begins to peek through the top of the meteorite as the gap between the two-piece widens. It must be working; the rock is separating. "Buckle up, men. We're going down."

Our ship begins to shake and the alert sounds. *'Red alert. Red alert.'* I stumble to a nearby seat and fasten the safety belt while my long braided black hair dangles perpendicular to my face. There's a loud cracking sound as the rock finally divides. Small stones hit our windshield as a clear view of Earth appears in front of us. There's a cheer from the crew, but it's short-lived. The power cuts out completely and we're free-falling toward a foreign planet. The crew scrambles to find somewhere to land. To avoid hitting anything, we plunge into the sea, submerging us in water. My seatbelt holds me in place as the force sucks the air out of my lungs. Our ship eventually settles on the top of the water while everyone breaks out in celebration.

"We did it," Captain Jinker shouts. Men clap and hug like one big happy family. I stay in my seat but allow myself to relax.

Once everyone calms, they turn their attention to me. I've never seen them act like this before and their faces turn serious as they stare at me. A few seconds tick by while I figure out my response. "Well done," I say, then smile, clapping my hands. The crew grin, showing they're happy with my actions, and I can breathe again.

One of the crew, Hix, brings up a picture of a flying object in the sky and audio fills the ship. "Come out slowly with your hands up." The interpreter chips under our skin automatically translate the words into our language. The voice sounds fierce and my *'well done'* now seems a small success compared to what I'm going to have to do next.

"What should we do, Captain?" Hix asks.

"I'm only in charge while this ship is flying. Prince Zenith is our leader while on Earth."

All eyes turn back to me. I might be a prince, but my father rules. I'm not usually given much responsibility. Dealing with a lack of space noodles is now looking appealing. At least that had an easy solution. Eat something else.

"Can we tap into their radio signal?" I ask.

"Yes. Just give me a little time," Hix says. He starts typing on the keyboard furiously.

Vehicles begin to land on an island close to our ship. Strobe lights flash through the windows and blind the cameras used to give us good peripheral vision. The sirens and demands continue until Hix finally gets us a direct link to the person in charge.

"You're speaking to Sergeant Carrie Jones. Who am I speaking with?" the voice says through the speaker.

I stand, moving closer to the communicator. "I'm Prince Zenith from the planet Kamath. There was a meteorite heading toward Earth. We took care of the situation." Captain Jinker assured me these creatures were intelligent. Did they think the life-threatening situation was resolved on its own? Did they even see it coming?

"The United States of America thanks you for your assistance. What is your reason for landing on the planet?"

"To destroy the meteorite, we had to use a lot of power. We need to recharge our batteries before we can leave."

"Is there anything we can do to help?" So far, they

haven't been overly welcoming, and I'm guessing they don't know what to make of us yet.

"No. The energy from the sun will help us on our way."

It takes her a few seconds to respond. "We'd like to meet you in person, Prince Zenith. Will you allow us to escort you to the New York police precinct?"

If I leave the comfort of my ship, I'll be opening myself up to following the rules of the planet. When studying the culture of humans, I learned a police precinct is a place of authority. Other than my father, people don't tell me what to do. "I think we should meet on neutral ground. We saved your planet. There's no need for all this dominance. You can call off your security."

A few more moments pass before we get an answer. The situation outside holds strong with no sign of anyone backing off. "Let's meet somewhere in the city. We could meet at a school or a coffee shop if you prefer."

A school is an education center for children. It shows she's putting some trust in me. The coffee shop is somewhere friends hang out. I believe it's a casual setting. "The school will be fine, but I'm happy to try the coffee."

"Excellent. I'll send directions, or do you need transportation?"

"Coordinates will be fine." We have a cruiser; a small spacecraft, and it will also give us an escape route.

Hix sets up the meeting and arranges our transportation. Captain Jinker stays with most of the crew. Humans stare at us as we pass through the streets above the traffic. The buildings are high, and we fly between them fast enough for them to blur together. There are so many people in such a small place. My home planet is underpopulated in comparison, and we have lots of woodland areas. We park on the roof and enter the school through the fire escape. We're met by the military before our feet hit the stairs. I follow in silence, taking in the building. The handrail is lower than I'd like and my surroundings make me feel tall. There's nothing usual about the education center.

Once we reach the meeting room, their security gestures for me to go inside. "Prince Zenith, it's nice to meet you." The voice comes from a petite older woman who must be the person I spoke to on the phone. She wears her hair tight to her head, whereas mine is braided down my back. The sternness in her expression shows the discipline of her youth. She's the woman who's going to find my Earthling match, she just doesn't know it yet.

"Sergeant Carrie Jones. It's a pleasure." I take her hand and kiss it like in the movies I've watched. She has guards with her, and they are watching my every move. I smile easily, hoping they get the message. *I'm not a threat.*

"I'll cut to the chase. We are truly grateful for your intervention. We did not have the situation under control and today would've been unfavorable without your help. While you're spending time in America, what are you expecting from us?"

I scrub my face. "You seem skeptical of me and my crew. You don't have to be. We come in peace. While here, I'd like a guide to show me what's good about this country."

"Within the American army, there are plenty of knowledgeable men who would be able to give you a tour." She points to the two guys on her left. They both remain motionless.

"No."

"No?" She frowns.

"I don't want a babysitter. I want someone about my age and female. A woman who lives in the city. I want an authentic experience, not someone who's watching me."

"How old are you? I'm not sure how things work on your planet, but how are you expecting me to find a guide at such short notice? Do you want me to put out an advert and see who responds?"

That sounds like a long process. I look around the room, seeing all the drawings from the children. "I'm twenty-five years old. Isn't there a teacher that could do it?" A young teacher about my age sounds perfect.

She nods. "Let me talk to the principal and I'll see what I can do."

My mission on Earth is finally on track. I will find my mate and get my ship back in the air. After the meeting, we return to the ship. The crew seems optimistic, and it feels good to be the man calling all the shots. I'm looking forward to meeting the human who will be assigned to me, but for now, I go to my quarters to rest.

CHAPTER THREE

Naomi

With everything that's happened in the last twenty-four hours, I shouldn't be so on edge about the school calling. Life has been put into perspective. Love and family are the things that matter most, but I want this job so freaking much.

"You can't sit around waiting for them to call. The world almost ended yesterday. We need to get out and enjoy life," Sonya says, hitting me with a pillow from the couch where I sit.

"When everything unraveled yesterday, all I could think was that I'd left my dad behind. In the light of day, I'm back to reality. I'm waiting for the call that could shape my career. It shouldn't feel that big a deal, but it does." I shrug. I've worked hard to get here and can't imagine swaying from my goal.

"Yes. It was pretty scary. I used to think living with my parents was holding me back. Now I realize a hug is more important than anything."

"Have you called them?" I've spoken to my dad a lot since yesterday. Probably more than the whole time I've lived here.

"Yes. We hugged on the phone, but it isn't the same." She smiles sadly.

"Did it make you see things differently?" I'd be sad to lose my roommate, but I'd understand if she wanted to move back to Brooklyn. Even I'd thought about going home. Deep down, my heart wants to be in New York.

"For sure it did. I wish I'd eaten the cream cake I wanted while having coffee yesterday." She smirks.

I laugh. "I get that. We should get the biggest cakes we can find and stuff our faces."

"The problem is, I'll have to work twice as hard in the gym tomorrow." She sighs heavily.

"I thought we were forgetting about tomorrows."

The amount of walking we do burns off enough calories for a treat every once in a while.

"I'll grab some cupcakes and wine in the store later and we'll have a girls' night."

"I like that idea."

My phone starts to ring from an unknown number. Sonya and I stare at each other. "Answer it."

We both cross our fingers. I accept the call with my heart in my throat. "Hello. Naomi speaking."

"Hi, Naomi. It's Mrs. Lionel from Greenview High."

"It's great to hear from you." I hold my breath, waiting for her to speak.

"I have a special assignment which I'm hoping you'll be interested in."

I frown. This is not how I thought this conversation was going to go. What could she possibly mean? "Okay. I'm listening."

"I'm guessing you've seen the visitors we have in New York. The aliens came to the school yesterday and the leader is looking for a tour guide. We need to do a background check and look at your references before you start teaching at the school.

I'm wondering if you'll consider this assignment while we wait. You will be paid for your time."

I try to process what she's saying. "I got the job?"

"Congratulations, Ms. Allen."

I let out a squeal and Sonya starts jumping in the air. It takes me a few seconds to calm down. "Sorry. Thank you so much. I could be a guide for a few days or weeks." I'm no expert on New York or cultural integrations, but I want to make a good impression on the school. The way she offered me the job made it sound like it was important. She should have started by telling me I was hired as a teacher. As a new starter, I knew there could be tasks given to me that nobody else wanted. I'm guessing this is the first one.

"Great. Can you be at the school in an hour or two?"

"Erm… yes." *That doesn't give me long to prepare.*

"Okay. Great. We'll see you then." She hangs up.

"So, tell me what she said," Sonya says.

It takes me a few seconds to process what I agreed to. "I have a teaching job and I'm going to be an alien tour guide." I give her my craziest stare. I've never given a human a city tour, never mind someone who's probably never visited our planet.

"That sounds fun. Where are you going to take them?" She doesn't seem fazed by my task.

I let out a strangled laugh. "How can you be taking this so casually?" My hair flops in front of my face and I drag it back with my hand. "This is insane. I have no idea what to show them."

"It's easy. Just do the touristy things."

"Okay. I can do that." I nod. Using my phone, I pull up an itinerary before getting my things together and heading to the school.

***

When I enter Greenview High, I take in the décor differently. Soon, it will be my students' work on the wall and one of these classrooms will be mine. The excitement is hard to contain. I make my way to the principal's office with a skip in my step and knock on the door. The voices inside stop talking and there is movement within the room. A military man eventually opens the door. All eyes turn to me, but it's the beautiful blue man with the huge muscles I can't stop staring at. His gaze latches onto mine and I can't look away. *He's mesmerizing.*

"Thank you for coming, Naomi. This is Sergeant Carrie Jones and her team," Mrs. Lionel says.

I smile at her, but before I get a chance to respond, the big blue guy walks towards me. People in the room tense like they're ready to take action if needed. It's almost laughable. For some reason, I instantly feel at ease with this guy. His chest is bare and his pants are tight. He doesn't seem to be hiding anything dangerous.

"Greetings. I'm Prince Zenith, but you can call me Zee." He takes my tiny hand, warming it with his. Lifting it, he brings it to his lips and places a lingering kiss on it.

"Hi, I'm Naomi," I say almost breathlessly. *What is wrong with me?* It's like Zee is taking up all the space in the room. "I'm your tour guide," I add, trying to pull back some of the control.

"It's nice to meet you, tiny human," he says and then grins. His purple eyes shine like clear amethyst stones. A cold shower would be good about now.

I pull a fake disgusted face and then swat his arm. "I'm not that small."

Someone gasps like I just did something

outrageous. The room seems to stand still as everyone takes in our interactions. Zee holds eye contact with amusement dancing across his features. I'm the first to look away. I finally notice the other alien who is a paler shade of blue. He seems ready to remove me from the room if Zee reacts badly to what just happened. The police and military presence also take a step closer. "Just tiny compared to me," Zee says, pulling my attention back to him.

"You are huge and so blue." *Please don't let my lack of sophistication lose me this job.*

"Thank you." He thrusts out his chest proudly.

I laugh, though my words weren't supposed to be a compliment. "You are welcome."

He takes my hand again. "So, let's go."

We both take a step toward the door. "Wait. We need to talk about security," Sergeant Jones says.

"I've already told you, Sergeant Carrie Jones. I come in peace," Zee says in an almost bored tone.

"I meant for you. It's not like you can hide your appearance and people will be curious about you."

"I'll figure it out." He opens the door, and we step

out.

"Wait, Prince Zenith," his fellow alien says.

"Hix, go back to the ship. I'm sure someone will give you a ride. I'm taking the cruiser."

"But, sir…" He runs after us. The panic in his voice is clear. "I should come with you."

"No. Go back to the ship."

He looks like he wants to argue further but thinks better of it. "Yes. Prince Zenith." He bows his head.

Zee is quiet as he leads me to the roof of the school. Maybe I should feel nervous to be alone with a stranger, but there's something about him that is calming. He holds the fire escape open for me and I step towards the gun-metal gray spaceship. This all feels unreal. When I imagined visitors from another world, the transportation is what I thought it would be, but I never thought I'd be physically attracted to someone that looks like him. His biceps tense as he pulls down the hatch and lifts me inside. He climbs in behind me and closes us off to the world.

"I thought we'd visit the Statue of Liberty, the Empire State Building, the Brooklyn Bridge, and maybe Central Park." I pull up the list I made on my phone.

"What are all those things?" He frowns.

"Places to visit when you're in New York." I show him a picture of the bridge.

"Are they places you go regularly?"

"No. They're tourist hotspots." Maybe I should've started with a history lesson or asked some questions about his knowledge.

"I want to see your life. The places you go."

That's not what I expected. My walk-up apartment isn't the sort of place I would take any visitors to. I don't even make my dad tackle the stairs. Since living here, I've been concentrating on finding a job. I've spent time in the coffee shops, but the grocery store is where I go the most. A little bit of me mixed with some touristy things is what I need. "I have an idea. Let's go to the aquarium in Coney Island."

"Okay."

He doesn't question my decision. Together, we map out our journey and take to the skies. Seeing the city from above is completely different. I sit in the seat next to Zee while trying to process what I've gotten myself into.

CHAPTER FOUR

Zenith

We're under the sea on land and I don't think I've ever seen so many fish. Naomi seems passionate about her surroundings. It's almost as good as seeing her in my space. Her smell is intoxicating. She's a burst of sweet wild berries and vanilla. From the second she walked into the education office, I knew she was my true mate by the way she smelt. Not just a potential match. She was literally made for me.

"Do you have fish on your planet?" Naomi asks.

"Of course."

"I'm curious about your home. You could live in the desert or somewhere nothing like Earth."

"Kamath is different. One day, maybe I can show you." Her eyes almost bulge, and I instantly realize I've made a mistake. It was too fast to even hint I might take her away from her home planet. "I mean show you a picture."

She smiles, recovering from her initial shock. "Yes. I'd love to see pictures."

"Great."

She pauses next to one of the large tanks. "You don't seem that into the fish. What type of tour were you wanting?"

"There is nothing wrong with the place you've brought me. I'm just not seeing why this place is important to you."

She touches her chest. "Me personally?"

"Yes."

"I grew up near the beach. My father is a big part of my life and he's a marine scientist. The fish are kind of like my friends."

"What are you doing in the city?" Since arriving, I haven't seen much wildlife. The buildings have taken over where the trees would've grown.

We move across to a nearby bench and sit down. "I'm in New York for my career. I trained to be a teacher and Greenview High gave me my first opportunity. The pace here is faster and that's what I'm used to. Places to relax are a little farther away. Visiting the aquarium is my special place." She sounds positive, but I'm sensing there's some underlying sadness. It's something I don't understand. I've done things I didn't want to for my people and my father, but never on this scale.

"You're ambitious." I nod.

"And you're not?"

"I'm a prince. My life is pretty much mapped out for me. All I need to solidify is my relationship with my mate."

"Oh. Is she blue like you?"

"There are no females of my species." I try to be vague because I don't want to scare her again. Her voice does have an edge to it, though. Could she be disappointed there might be someone else for me?

"Okay, so let's finish walking around the aquarium and grab a coffee."

"Coffee. Yes. Why not." We drink juice from the

plants back home, but I'm willing to try this strange beverage.

We move to the café, and I can feel the eyes of the humans on me, but all I can focus on is Naomi. "Do you want a latte, americano, cappuccino, or a flat white?"

The chalkboard names all these things as coffee. From what I've heard, there's not that much difference between them. "Whatever you choose will be fine."

"Hmm." She nods.

"What?"

"I had you as a decisive guy. Never did I think you'd let someone else choose."

"I'll handle the big things, but since I know nothing about Earth beverages, I'll leave it in your capable hands."

She bites her lip like she's trying to figure me out. After a few seconds, she leaves me at the table and goes to order. When she comes back, she has two paper cups. One says *Naomi* on it, and the other says *the big blue guy*. I smirk. Is that the main thing she sees about me? Unable to stop myself, I sit up taller and thrust out my chest. Her eyes drop down my body and wander over my muscles appreciatively. The attraction is there. That cup should say *hot blue guy*. She gives me my drink and I bring it up to my lips to taste it. The boiling liquid burns my throat, making me choke.

She gets to her feet, racing to my side of the table. Her soft hands rest on my shoulders. "Oh, gosh. I should've warned you. It needs time to cool down."

"Is this really a favorite American pastime?"

"Most people would say that's baseball or basketball. Sports."

"But not you?"

"I don't mind games." She shrugs indifferently.

Humans seem complex. There are so many layers I need to peel back with her. So far, I don't think my approach is working. We seem completely different, yet she smells like my mate. We should fit. In my head, I'd imagined her to be swooning over my every word, but I was mistaken. Even though our day together has been okay, it hasn't been life-changing.

We drink our coffee, which will not be my new

addiction, and by the time we're heading back to the cruiser, I'm ready to call it a day.

I help her into the ship before closing the hatch. Once it's powered up, the communication light comes on. Someone has been trying to reach me. At first, I ignore it and take to the sky. It doesn't take long for a constant ringing to start.

"What is that noise?" Naomi asks.

"The main ship is trying to communicate with us."

"Aren't you going to answer them?"

We look at each other for a few seconds. *What could be so urgent that they couldn't wait for me to get back to them?*

I answer by pressing the accept button. "Hello, Captain," I say, presuming it's him.

"Prince Zenith, we have a problem," he says in a shaky voice.

"Go ahead. You can speak freely."

"Is the human still with you?"

"Yes, but it's okay." Although we haven't found that magic spark yet, I trust whatever he has to say will be okay for her to hear.

"The Rabot seems to have followed us here and is requesting to land on Earth."

My heart begins to race. My uncle's fleet is our enemy, and there's no reason for his ship to be here. Nothing good ever happens when he's around.

"Have they made contact with us yet?"

"Not yet, sir."

I'm my father's only heir. If they get to me, my uncle could stake claim to the throne. "I'll find somewhere to lie low for a while. Then when we have a better understanding of the situation, you can call me on the mobile communicator." This could potentially be a life-threatening situation.

"Good plan."

"Goodbye." I hang up.

Naomi bites her nail. "Should we be worried?"

I wrap my arm around her shoulders to offer comfort. "No. The Earthlings will be safe. It's me they want."

The unease on her face deepens into a frown. "What will they do?"

"They have to find me before we have to think about that." She seems to care about me, which is a good sign.

"If you haven't noticed, you don't exactly blend in." She's the second person to remind me of that. I am not meant to go unseen. I'm a prince and from a different land. Usually, this would be something to be proud of. Yet it might be my downfall in trying to avoid my uncle. The only advantage is I'm going to take the opportunity to get to know Naomi on a deeper level.

"I'm sure you'll find somewhere for me to hide."

"Me?" She touches her chest in disbelief.

"Unless you'd rather I explore the city in my cruiser and walk along with the humans while I look for somewhere?" Adding that last bit might've been a little too much, but I want her to think about me. Usually, it's the alpha male that protects their females. I'm going to see what my female can do for me. Hopefully, it will bring us closer.

"That's not going to work. Did you see all the women staring at you in the aquarium?" She crosses her arms, and I wonder if she might be a tiny bit jealous. *One can hope.*

"Will you help me?"

She looks off into the distance before pulling up coordinates on her electronic device. "I have an idea," she says, looking back at me.

"Lead the way." I gesture to the control panel.

Her smile is wicked. "You'll let me drive?"

I pause before answering. This is an opportunity to get physically close to her, but she's obviously never piloted a spacecraft before.

How bad could it be?

"Sure," I tell her. She stands in front of me, and I lean closer to her ear. "This is the throttle. Ease into the movement." I put my hand over hers. An electrical pulse vibrates up my arm. This is the kind of connection I was hoping for. I show her how to insert the destination and the steering. I linger closer than necessary. She smells too good.

"Everything looks so much clearer up here." Her voice comes out raspy.

"Yes. It does." Together, we follow the coordinates

and fly off into the night.

CHAPTER FIVE

Naomi

Zee will be the first guy I've brought home to meet my dad and he's not even my boyfriend. We pull a khaki green waterproof cover over the cruiser, leaving it tucked away in the shared garden area. The parrot squawks as we walk past its cage. Zee stops to look at it while I continue to the back door.

I pull back the fly net and shout through to my dad. "Hi, it's Naomi. Are you home?"

"Naomi? What are you doing here?" My dad appears in the hallway.

I start with the good news before springing the bigger stuff on him. "I got the job at the school."

He walks towards me and wraps his arms around me. "That's great. I was so worried about you. I'm glad you came."

A lot has happened in the last twenty-four hours. I'd almost forgotten about the meteorite. "It's good to see you." I hug him tightly.

We break apart, and he frowns. "My old work friends are skeptical about what's happening with our invaders. Another spacecraft has breached the Earth's atmosphere. The second ship is more suspicious, and we've started monitoring the skies."

"I thought most of your friends were marine based." My dad is retired and probably has too much time on his hands. He seems invested in the details of the invasion.

"Yes, but something like this means we're pulling resources. We have a few specialists…" His voice trails off.

The door squeaks as it opens, and my dad's eyes widen when Zee enters. The silence is deafening as we stand staring at each other. My mouth feels dry, and I swallow the lump in my throat. "Now, Dad, don't freak out. This is Prince Zenith. There's no need to be scared. He's good, I promise. Zenith, this is my dad, Ralph."

Zee gets on one knee and lowers his head. "It's an honor to meet you."

He's never greeted anyone like this before. I wonder what makes my dad so special. I would've thought a prince would expect this kind of greeting, not to get down on one knee himself.

"See? He's fine," I say, trying to shrug off whatever is happening here.

Dad steps closer to him. "You're so blue."

"Yes. I am aware of that." Zee gets to his feet, towering over him.

"And big."

I tap my dad's shoulder to reassure him. "Now we've established he's big and blue, let's go into the living room so we can talk."

Zee must think we're all a bit simple. I think my greeting was similar to my dad's. The two obvious facts about this man are not all he is. I haven't figured him out yet, but I know he's good.

My dad makes us some drinks and we sit on the

couches. Zee takes up most of the space on the one we're sharing. My dad pushes his glasses up his nose. "What brought you to Earth?"

"My crew saw the meteorite, and we decided we could help." Zee sounds surprised by his answer. His words come out unevenly like he's realizing something as he says them.

"Why were you in the vicinity of our planet in the first place?" My dad's tone is harsh, as though he's accusing him of something.

"We were passing by."

"Hmm." My dad gives a false smile. He doesn't believe him, and it makes me want to defend Zee.

"It's the second spaceship we need to be wary of," I say, confirming my dad's early theory.

"What makes you say that?" He rubs his chin like he's trying to figure out what I'm thinking.

"It's my uncle's fleet. My father is the king, and my uncle, his younger brother, wishes he was. The other ship is a threat to me."

"That's why we're here. We need your help to stay under the radar while we figure out what's going on," I say.

My dad scratches the back of his head. "Okay. I'll call the guys and we'll come up with a plan."

"No. For now, I think we should keep this between us." I feel protective of Zee. The fewer people who know where we are, the better.

"Okay. For now, we'll do it your way, but I'm warning you, Zee. If you hurt my daughter in any way, I'll make sure you pay for it."

Woah. Dad has never threatened any of my friends before. What did he mean by any way? What could Zee possibly do to hurt me?

Zee nods his head. "Understood."

We have our evening meal together and my dad drops the hostile act as he begins to relax around our guest. He shows him some of his fish before leaving him with Bill the parrot. Zee seems to really like the bird. My dad signals for me to meet him in the hallway. "I hope you know what you're doing."

"You have to trust me, Dad." Zee doesn't make me nervous. If anything, he settles me. Once my dad spends more time with him, he'll see what I do too.

He hugs me. "I do."

We pull the spare bedding out of the closet, and I

help my dad set up a makeshift bed on one of the couches. We say our goodnights and he leaves me with Zee. I step outside and find him exactly where I expected. He's still admiring the bird.

"It's not perfect, but we've put a bed together for you on the couch."

"Where will you be sleeping?"

"This is my childhood home. I have a room."

"Can I see it?"

Instinct wants me to say no. I wasn't part of a team or a club that I have plastered all over the wall, but that doesn't mean my space isn't personal. My apartment in New York is minimal, but my bedroom here is full of my childhood choices. "Why do you want to look at it?"

"I want to see everything that is yours."

The way he says it leaves me feeling bare, like he's talking about more than my materialistic possessions. A warm blush creeps up my face. Zee isn't wearing much clothing and it doesn't leave a lot to the imagination. I'm not sure if it's a reflection of his personality, but I trust he's not hiding anything from me. I can grant him this small insight. "Just a quick peek."

I lead him down the hall while my nerves jumble in my stomach. My hand grasps the handle of the door to my room, and I hesitate before turning it. Slowly, the door glides open revealing too much pink and fluffy material. In high school, I was proud of my girliness. Now, I'm wishing I'd been one of the popular people who wanted a grown-up room.

Zee seems mesmerized by my things as he takes everything in. He touches the teddies long forgotten on the shelf and works his way down to my drawers.

I put my hand over the underwear drawer before he can open it. "Not that one," I say, shaking my head.

"What's so important I can't see it?"

"A lady's underwear is personal. We don't show it to just anyone." I widen my eyes to emphasize my words.

"Maybe one day I'll see."

My face burns. I'm not sure if we're understanding each other correctly. Luckily, he can't read my thoughts. Zee is very good-looking, and it's been a while since I focused on anything other than getting a job. I'd like to know what it would be like to kiss those luscious blue lips. An image of him covering me with his huge body flashes before my eyes. My temperature starts to rise at the thought of being intimate with him.

But he's going to leave Earth eventually. I'm starting my dream of being a teacher. There's no future for us long-term, so I should shut these thoughts down now. Would one night with him really be so bad, though?

"It's intimate," I explain. "Like for couples."

"It's for mates to see?" He thrusts out his chest. My eyes shamelessly wander over his muscles. I've never openly checked a guy out before, but I can't help myself.

"Sure. Mates." I nod.

He starts to walk towards the door. "So, it's for another day."

I stumble behind him. Did we misunderstand each other, or did he just hit on me? Usually, if a guy is flirting, they wouldn't be fleeing the room. A tingle starts in my core. Maybe I want him to show an interest in me.

He moves to the couch and lies down. I put the blanket over him in case he's unsure what he should be doing. He fluffs the pillow.

"I guess this is goodnight," I say.

"Goodnight, my favorite human."

A warm feeling settles in my stomach, and I smile. "Supposing you haven't met many people, I don't have much competition. Thanks anyway." My words were supposed to lighten the mood and get my mind out of the gutter. Somehow, I just sound nervous.

I'm not sure if he knows I can hear him, but he replies as I leave, "It wouldn't matter how many humans I met. You're the one."

My heart flutters, but I don't turn around. Once alone in my room, I allow myself to relax. There's an alien sleeping on my couch. He's giving off all kinds of vibes and it's affecting me in all kinds of ways.

CHAPTER SIX

Zee

I look in the garden for something to make for breakfast. We're close to the ocean, but I'm not sure if the fish are for food or friends only. Staying close to the house, I find a tree with fruit. I tightly grip the trunk, pulling myself up to the top. Removing the knife from my boot, I cut the light green fruit off before carrying it down to the ground. I repeat the process a couple more times.

The back door opens, and Naomi appears in a long bunny shirt and matching slippers. "Zee. What are you doing? Someone might see you. Get inside now," she scolds.

I grab one last piece of fruit before climbing down.

"Good morning."

She picks up two of the fruits. "Come on." I follow her. "Why are you collecting coconuts?"

"Breakfast. Don't you eat in the morning?"

"We have a fridge full of food. There's no need to work so hard."

I frown. Naomi isn't easily impressed. My efforts need to be doubled if I'm going to make her swoon. While she cooks in the kitchen, I use my device to search for uses for coconuts. The kind I've picked are best for drinks. With my knife, I jab a hole in the side so I can release the juice into a jug I find on the counter.

"Morning," Ralph says when he joins us.

"Greetings," I say.

"Good morning. I've made omelets and Zee got us some fresh coconut water," Naomi adds.

Her dad observes the fruit I've massacred. Finding some glasses, I pour him a drink, along with one for myself and another for Naomi. He frowns as I push the glass toward him. "I didn't buy any coconuts from the store," he says.

"Zee got them from the palm tree in the garden."

"Did anyone see him?" He sounds as angry as Naomi did. It's early and I was stealthy. There's no need for them to worry.

"I don't think so." She shakes her head.

They are talking like I'm not here. I'm not used to people questioning my judgment. Her dad doesn't seem to be completely accepting of me, yet he's worried for my safety. His opinion is important as I feel it will matter to my mate. From the information I have on marriage, a father's approval is essential to winning over the female.

"I wanted to help with breakfast," I say.

"It was kind of you, but we need to keep a low profile." Naomi places the food in front of us and we settle at the table.

"Have you had contact with your crew yet?" Ralph asks me.

"I'm going to check in with my men after the food."

Naomi picks up a fork and I watch how she picks up her egg. I copy her. The texture of the egg is foreign to my tongue. It tastes okay. The coconut liquid is not so great. I'm now understanding why humans drink coffee.

I have my mobile communication device, however, I want a few minutes to myself. Using one of Naomi's blankets to hide under, I make my way to the cruiser. Once alone, I call for an update.

"Captain Jinker, what's your status?"

"Prince Zenith, it's good to hear your voice. We've had no contact with the enemy ship yet. If they know we're here, they haven't made it known."

"Keep me posted."

"Will do." There's a noise in the background of the mothership.

"What was that?" I ask.

"I'm not sure yet. The crew is looking into it. Have you found a mate?"

"Yes." There's another sound, only this time it's louder. Is there trouble on the ship?

"Hold on, sir."

I can hear running and shouting. "Jinker?" The line goes dead. "Jinker?" I hit redial, but there's no response. The thud of my heart is uncontrollable. I pound my fist against the control panel.

Fuck. I should never have left them. Firing up the cruiser, I'm ready to leave when Naomi comes out, waving her arms.

I open the hatch. In the panic, I almost left her behind.

"Where are you going?" she asks.

"Something has happened to my men. I need to go back to see if I can help." I can't hide how frantic I feel.

"I thought you were hiding. You can't go into a dangerous situation with no backup or understanding of what's going on." She folds her arms across her chest. She's angry I was leaving.

"What do you suggest I do?" I'm not a coward. Leaving the mothership was a mistake. I could've done something.

"We need to watch the news."

I stop preparing the cruiser, ready to understand her plan. "What's that?"

"If something has happened in New York, there will be a report. Come inside and I'll show you." I step out of my ship. We move closer and she holds my hand. Her forehead is wrinkled, and she looks worried. *Does she care for me?*

"Show me."

She nods before wrapping her arms around me and pulling me into a hug. She smells even better up close. Some of my panic subsides now I have her in my arms.

We go inside the house, but I don't let go of her hand. She switches on an electronic box and listens to what the human has to say. A clip of my ship submerging underwater after being attacked is played. We watch the scene over and over but don't find out any new information.

"It's time we get some outside help," Ralph says.

"It's too risky," Naomi replies.

"Do you have a better plan?" They stare at each other for a few seconds before turning to me.

I'm not used to feeling out of control. If I go to the ship without a method to retrieve my ship or any security, I could be walking into a trap. I might lose more than I already have. Naomi is my mate whether she knows it or not. I have to trust she couldn't put me in danger. Her father might not like me yet, but he can't deny there's a connection between us. She's gripping my hand so tight and looking as worried as I feel. I've got to have faith in her and her family. I shake my head. "I don't know what we should do."

"I'll call the guys," her dad says.

Naomi hesitates but eventually nods. "Okay."

He goes into the kitchen, and I pull Naomi down onto the nest I made last night. She allows me to wrap my arms around her. There's a chance I'm stranded on Earth. There's no way the cruiser will make it back to my home planet, and what about my crew? They are good men. The journey here might have softened my tough exterior. I care about my people, and if I can save them, I'll do everything in my power to secure their safety. It's me my uncle wants, not them.

Without a mate, my planet is a dying race. That's the whole reason we've come to Earth. Naomi is the one for me. I can feel it deep in my soul. Sacrificing my crew is a big price to pay for love. I just hope, somehow, they're still alive.

CHAPTER SEVEN

Naomi

Our living room is full of ex-marines and retired scientists. They're talking so fast I'm struggling to keep up. Zee seems to like their optimism, and from what I understand, everyone seems to be predicting where the ship is.

Grayson, my dad's friend, says, "I think we should form two teams and search the River Hudson."

Martin adds, "These look like the most likely search areas."

The army is in the area which is reported as a no-flight area on the news. Chaos seems to be the main message, yet my dad's friends don't seem to be fazed. They talk strategy while Zee tries to communicate with his ship.

Dad pulls me into the kitchen. "We need to talk."

"What's up?"

"My friends are ready to put themselves on the line to help the aliens. I need to make sure you trust they're telling the truth. We don't want to get in the middle of a war that's nothing to do with us."

"I haven't known him long, but there's something about him. My gut feeling is we need to help them. They saved us from the meteorite. This is our way to repay the favor. Zee has given me no reason to doubt them. Why are you hesitating to believe him?" Zee needs to win my dad over. If we had more time, I'm sure they would like each other. For now, he'll have to trust me.

He rubs his hand over his face. "I've seen the way he looks at you."

"What does that mean?" I frown.

"He's interested in you and it's a little intimidating."

My dad telling me someone is crushing on me is a little strange. We've never been open about relationships and I've never introduced a potential boyfriend before. I've dated plenty but never got serious with anyone enough to bring them home to meet my dad. "Why is it frightening?"

"That's not the word I used."

"What's the problem?" Zee's a big guy, but I don't think that's what he means either.

"He's just not what I expected for you."

"Firstly, nothing has happened between Zee and me. We've only just met. Secondly, no girl thinks they'll end up dating an alien." I laugh nervously.

"Be truthful with me. How do you see this ending?"

"Zee will go back to his home planet, and I'll start my new job."

He hugs me. "As long as you're being realistic. Okay, let's go help the big blue guy." I shake my head as we walk back into the room. Dad still hasn't called him by his name.

"It's decided, then. We'll fly to the old marine base and take the submarines," Martin says.

"What teams have you split into?" Dad asks.

"It makes sense for us to have a range of skills on each boat."

A few of them nod in agreement.

"What about Zee and me?" I ask.

Everyone turns to look at me. "You guys need to stay here," Grayson says.

Zee stands abruptly. "It will be safer for Naomi if she stays here. You can't leave me behind, though."

"I'm not staying here," I say.

"If you come, Prince Zenith, you'll put us all in extra danger. We can't risk it," Martin says.

Zee takes a step forward like he's ready to argue. "It's my men and my ship. I should be there for them."

"We understand your loyalty, but we have to do the best for everyone. Plus, where do you see my daughter in this situation? She needs someone to stay with her as I won't put her in the direct firing line. She's safe here. Nobody is looking for you in Florida, and together, I think you'll look out for each other," Dad says.

The conversation in the kitchen is about more than looking for the ship. My dad is trying to figure out our relationship. If he's willing to leave us together, he must see a deep connection.

Zee rubs his face in frustration before looking down at his feet. "Okay." I don't think he's used to giving others control over important decisions.

Some more of the details are hashed out. Zee and I stay close as I try to comfort him. Once the plan is in place, we say our goodbyes to the group before sitting together in the quiet aftermath.

"How are you feeling?" I ask.

"It's hard to sit back and allow someone else to hold the reins."

"Who was in charge while you were in space? Didn't the captain give the orders?"

He bites his lip. "Yes. He had the initial control, but overall, the decisions were mine."

I caress the back of his hand. "He will have done the best he could."

"You're right. It's just a difficult situation to be in."

"We'll have to keep busy while we wait for

information. We can watch the news for updates. Hopefully, it will keep us in the loop until we know what to do."

He slides his fingers along my wrist. "What do you have in mind?"

My pulse quickens. He looks deep into my eyes. This wasn't what I was thinking, but now his lips look tempting. His hand wanders up to mine, and I lean in. Our lips meet, and it's electric. He tastes of honey and citrus. His arms wrap around me, and he pulls me close. "It'll be okay."

"Thank you for having faith." Our first kiss is perfect, and he doesn't push for more. We watch the news while cuddling on the couch. Unfortunately, we don't get any new information. I fit perfectly against Zee's side, and it feels good. I'm not sure if it's the heightened energy of the situation or exhaustion, but we fall asleep.

***

It's dark when we wake. Instantly, I check my phone for messages. The TV is still playing but nothing has changed. As I look at Zee, he seems vulnerable. He's no longer just this huge blue guy with a beautiful face. He's a man with a world on his shoulders.

His eyes flutter open. "What are you staring at?" Zee asks.

"You." I lick my lips. We hold eye contact while lust sizzles between us. One taste is all I need. He leans in and kisses me. It's soft and sensual. This guy is giving me feelings I've never had before and it's scary how fast I'm craving him. It's like we have this special bond where logic is thrown out of the equation. The kisses deepen and he pulls me closer. I slide onto his knee, straddling his waist. My hands explore his chest as he strokes my hair. "Wow. This feels so right."

"Of course it does. You are mine." Confidence reaps from his words.

Butterflies erupt in my stomach. He sounds so alpha possessive; it's a turn-on. Heat rushes through my body and tingles down my spine. Instead of acting cautiously, I'm ready to jump in. Seeing his vulnerable side has changed things. The stakes are high and I'm going to live recklessly in the moment. I don't know how much time we'll have together, and I want to make the most of it. I'm ready to take the next step. My body glides over his as we start to grind together. I can feel his hard-on under his trousers and my panties dampen. A fever begins to take over me as my long skirt bunches around my waist. I've never been this forward. He touches the bare skin on my thighs, heating me from within. An uncontrollable moan leaves my mouth. "Zee."

"Yes, my mate."

His alien terminology is hot. He makes me feel like I'm the only one for him.

"You're burning up," I say. His body temperature is rising, and the blue of his skin is darkening into purple.

"Only for you, baby."

I'm finding it hard to concentrate between kisses. Does he know he's changing color?

The fastening on his trousers springs open and the head of his cock pokes through. I'm soaking wet as the folds of my pussy moisten further. I grind down on the tip of his erection. "Do you think we should take this to the bedroom?"

"Your nest?"

That's the first time I've heard it called that before. "Yes."

He picks me up like I weigh nothing and carries me down the hall. He opens the door with one hand, taking us into the room. We collapse onto the bed before he pulls back to remove his trousers. His huge cock stands to attention. It's ribbed from tip to base. There's a spill of pre-cum on the end and I lick my lips in anticipation. Zee is driving me crazy with lust. He reaches for me, pulling down my skirt and panties in one swift move. I lift my top off and remove my bra. He stares lustfully at my naked body. I'd be embarrassed if I wasn't shamelessly doing the same thing. "You're beautiful."

"Thank you."

"Now we will mate?"

I frown, but it fades as he kisses up my neck. Does he mean we're going to have sex or something more? My thoughts get lost and I find myself agreeing. "Yes. Give it to me."

He lines up his cock with my entrance. He looks into my eyes as he thrusts into me. The ripples of his cock massage the inside of my pussy. My nipples harden and a burst of pleasure erupts through me. He doesn't give me time to recover before he's pulling out and entering me again. Waves of euphoria pulse through me. I grip his shoulder as he kisses my lips with all he has. He fucks me hard and fast. The ribbed shape of his penis increases my enjoyment. It isn't long until I'm screaming his name. His skin glows purple. Everything about the way he touches me feels unique, and it doesn't take me long to orgasm again. He keeps up his pace until he empties his seed inside me.

"You are now mine," he says while softly stroking the sensitive skin behind my ear. The way he keeps repeating the words is mesmerizing, and even though I don't fully understand, I feel what he's saying is true.

Once he withdraws from inside me, we snuggle up in bed. He stays close and I feel protected. "Tell me about your planet," I say.

"What do you want to know?" He strokes my shoulder, and I'm so content I could purr.

"Tell me your favorite thing to do."

He keeps exploring my skin and it feels amazing. "We have a lake called Wisdom. It glows the color of the sun and it's said if you bathe in it, the gods might answer one of your life questions."

"Wow. That sounds magical." It's hard to imagine

his planet. It sounds like a natural beauty with less urbanization.

"It is. When the stars are setting in the sky just before dawn, it's the most tranquil place in Kamath."

"Do you go there often?" I'd love to see the place he's describing.

"Only when I dreamt of my mate."

"Do you have more than one in a lifetime?"

"No."

Butterflies erupt in my stomach. Does he mean he dreamt of me?

"What did you imagine when you thought of your mate?" It's too early for me to refer to myself as his mate. We've only slept together once.

"Trust me, the reality outweighs the fantasy." He kisses my lips, and instead of being scared, I'm excited to explore what our relationship means.

CHAPTER EIGHT

Zee

Last night, I mated with Naomi and showed my true color. Royal purple is a trait of my bloodline and a sign I've joined with my true partner. The glow has faded, but my skin holds the new coloring. We made love over and over last night. This morning, she smells of me. A satisfied grin creeps onto my face. I can't deny I'm happy, although I feel guilty. It's hard to be happy when there is uncertainty about my ship.

Leaving her in bed, I go to check the communication devices. The TV is spinning the same tale as last night and my cell isn't getting any response. I can't work Naomi's phone, so I don't explore the foreign technology. What if I'm stuck here? The thought should be terrifying, but now I have my mate, it doesn't seem so bad. Naomi told me she wants to be a teacher, and although typically the men bring home the food in Kamath, I could raise our children. My own future is second to hers because she's what I want most. I try to picture our home with our family. Florida is more family-friendly. A big garden and lots of space to run around sounds great.

"I wondered where you'd gone," Naomi says, interrupting my thoughts. She's wearing a long t-shirt and I'm disappointed she's covered up.

"No news from the TV or my crew," I say, holding up the remote. I've learned so much about Earth technology already.

She checks her phone. "My dad is in New York, but no luck yet." She smiles sadly, and I kiss her softly on the lips.

"I still have hope."

"Me too." She hugs me. "Shall we make breakfast?"

"Should I get some coconuts?"

"How about we stick to coffee?"

"That sounds perfect." Already, I have a preference. If I have to adjust for my mate, I'm willing to try my hardest.

She leads me into the kitchen. "I think you should put some pants on."

"Why? I have nothing to hide."

"Because you're too distracting."

"Oh, yeah?" I smile, liking her answer. She rolls her eyes, but she's wearing a grin that says she doesn't mind. A rush of blood hardens my cock and I'm ready to service my mate once more. I wrap my arms around her and she cuddles back into me. The edge of her shirt lifts as I embrace her. My erection touches her bare skin and I can smell her arousal. We kiss passionately as she turns to face me. I lift her onto the counter and she spreads her legs so she can draw me in close. We continue to make out while she grinds up against me. The tip of my cock nudges her entrance.

"You are very beautiful."

"And you are a bad influence."

"Only with you."

She smiles happily. "I like the way you say that."

"You are mine and I'm yours."

I thrust into her, making her moan in pleasure. "Oh, Zee. Yes."

Her words are what I want to hear, although I'm doubtful she understands just yet. I pull her as close as I can and we continue to explore each other's bodies. Her hair and skin are soft and delicate. I knead her neck through her hair while watching her nipples harden through the thin material of her clothing. We have the same idea, but she beats me to it. The shirt is gliding over her head like I wished it to disappear. My hand grips her perfect breast as I kiss along her jawline. She hooks her heels into the back of my legs, pulling me deeper inside her. I continue to fuck her, giving in to my animalistic urges. My seed begins to leak inside her and I don't hold back. It's like an eruption explodes inside her. Every last drop of my load spills into her and my cock pulses until I'm done.

We kiss a few more times before I help her down from the counter. "Do you still want me to put my pants on?" I ask.

She glances down, appreciating my body. "I'm afraid so." She pats my butt as I leave the room to retrieve them. When I return, she's covered herself up and the smell of coffee is in the air.

"Tell me what to do," I say.

She gives me a wicked smile. My mate has a playful side. "The coffee's brewing. It won't be long. Would you like to learn how to cook some human food?"

"Sure. Maybe one day I can return the favor and teach you how to make a Kamath-style breakfast."

"I'd like that." We kiss again.

She shows me how to fry sausages and eggs. Other than removing the shell on the egg, the process is fairly straightforward. I pour the coffee into cups, and when the food is ready, we sit at the table to eat. "This is good, right?"

"Yes. There's no need to catch your breakfast when you have a fridge."

She laughs. "So, if you were teaching me how to prepare food on your planet, would I be expected to climb trees first? I'm not sure I could even do that."

"The best fruit is the freshest." I would gather the fruit if I needed to. The idea of having her in my space is arousing.

"What would we have with the fruit?" She sounds genuinely interested in my planet, and I like it.

"Milk from the animals."

"Straight from the source?"

"Absolutely."

We finish our food before going back into the living room. Naomi's cell starts to ring. Quickly, she grabs it and answers. "Hello. Dad?"

"Yes, it's me." His voice is quiet, but I can still hear him.

"Have you found anything?"

"We've made contact."

I move closer to Naomi. My heart is pounding in my chest. *Please let them be alive.* "Do you know what happened?"

"They've sustained damage from the enemy ship but didn't have enough power to set off, so they chose to sink the ship."

"Is everyone okay?"

"Yes, they're fine. They're going to need help moving to a safer location. We've already been in touch with the army, and they've agreed to help."

"What about Zee's uncle?"

"There's no sign of him, but he hasn't left the planet."

"Be careful."

"You too. I love you."

"I love you too. Goodbye."

"Goodbye."

The communication ends.

"My men are okay. This is a good day." Words can't express the relief I feel.

"Yes." We smile at each other before diving into an uncontrollable kissing session. The heat from before is back, only this time, it's sweeter.

"Zee."

Naomi's face pales. The fire between us dies out. Happiness vanishes from Naomi's face as she points to the TV. The news people have shifted location. Instead of reporting from the mothership, my small cruiser is being uncovered.

"I think we have a problem."

CHAPTER NINE

Naomi

Racing around the house, we quickly cover all the windows and doors. "I wonder how they found us," I say.

I accidentally knock over a lamp and spill a glass of abandoned water. My bottom lip wobbles with worry. A target has been put on our heads, and I'm scared. Mainly for Zee, but also for myself. Humans will show up here, which will lead to more attention. It won't be long until we're discovered. The enemy aliens might come for him.

"It doesn't matter. We need to get you to safety." He puffs out his chest, surrounding me with his big arms. It should offer me comfort, but if Zee's having negative thoughts, it can't be good.

Panic sets in as my pulse quickens. He said only I need to get to safety. What about him? I don't want us to be separated. "You can't leave me."

"That isn't an option." Relief immediately floods me. He's always seemed protective of me. Could there be a stronger bond than I thought? Is he feeling as connected to me as I do to him?

"We need a plan. Your cruiser isn't far from here and it won't take them long to move up to the house." We need to be smart. All lustful thoughts are cleared from my head. I'm ready to focus on keeping Zee safe. He might be protective of me, but I feel the same way about him.

"We need a distraction. My ship is the best way for us to escape." He brushes his fingers over my arm in a caring way. It's comforting, yet in his stern expression, I can see his attention is on what he has to do.

I've also got to do what's necessary to keep us out of the way of danger. "Maybe we should separate for a short time so I can lead them away."

"No. We're not splitting up." His tone leaves no room for arguments. If the situation weren't so urgent, I'd be all over him.

I'm not hopeful I can change his mind, but I have to try. If anything happens to him because of me, I couldn't forgive myself. "I don't want to lose you either, but it might be for the best."

"We are mated now. That isn't an option. My color has changed. He will be looking for you as much as me."

My mouth hangs open. I thought his purpleness was like a seasonal thing. "So, that's why you're no longer blue. Will everyone on your ship know we had sex?"

"Yes."

I start to blush but quickly shake my thoughts. "If we didn't have bigger things to be worrying about, I'd be embarrassed right now. We should get you a shirt and a hat so we can disguise all of your alienness and find somewhere to lie low until we can get to the ship."

"I agree."

Raiding my dad's wardrobe, I find a fishing hat and a marine life jumper. Once we've covered Zee up and I've got dressed, we take my dad's car to the docks. I manage to find an open shipping container and we go inside, leaving the door ajar.

I make a call to my dad and he picks up on the first ring. "I've just seen the reporters at our house. It isn't safe for you to stay there. You need to get out of there before it's too late." His words are rushed and urgent. It's obvious he's as unnerved as us.

"We'd already seen the news and we've moved down to the docks."

"Did you take my car? What if someone followed you?" He scolds me like I'm a child.

"Relax. I've parked in a container and we're out of sight." He's overreacting. We slipped out of the house without any problems.

"I'm going to send someone from the army to pick you both up."

My calm is soon shattered when the door to the shipping container is pushed shut and we're plummeted into darkness. My phone loses reception and the line goes dead. I pull it away from my ear and use the light to look around.

"I thought you said we would be alone here." I'm not sure what Zee thinks has happened.

"This is bad," I say. We try to open the door, but it's no use. He tries his communicator but the container blocks the signal. There's a noise and the ground begins to move. We're being lifted into the air. "I think we should sit in the car so we don't get crushed."

"Okay." He helps me into the car first before getting in. The handbrake is on and we sit tight as the contents of my stomach jumbles.

"Do you think it's your uncle that has us?"

"I don't know."

I bite my lip, trying to hold in the worry. "I'm scared."

"I'll take care of you." Zee pulls me into his arms and we kiss. Having him here does make me feel safer.

We seem to be in the air for a long time until eventually, we touch solid ground. All we can do is sit and wait to see who opens the container.

***

We've been screaming, trying to open the door, kissing, and eventually fell asleep. If I didn't have my phone, I'd have lost all sense of time. The squeak of the door has us both jumping to attention and the first bit of light is blinding. We both exit the car, moving towards the door.

"Hello, Uncle," Zee says, and my heart sinks.

"Prince Zenith, so good to see you." We step outside and are greeted by a group of less good-looking aliens. The features that make Zee look friendly are absent, although they're all muscular. I glance around, taking in the scenery. We seem to be in an industrial area away from the ocean. "And who might you be?" he asks me.

"She is mine and no concern of yours," Zee says.

"We'll see about that." His uncle walks over to me to take a closer look, and Zee growls. An evil laugh erupts from the pit of his uncle's stomach. He eyes me curiously for a few more minutes then turns his attention back to Zee. "I hear you're having a bit of engine trouble."

"Nothing that can't be fixed. We don't need your help, so you can leave," Zee says bitterly. There's no love between these two men.

"Now, now, young man. What kind of uncle would I be if I didn't help out my nephew?" He isn't sincere. I can feel it deep in my bones.

"You'd be a good uncle if you left me alone. My dad won't be impressed you're meddling in his business." Zee folds his arms.

"What was your purpose for traveling so far from home?" He glances at me again.

"That's none of your business." They hold eye contact for a few seconds.

He turns back to me and lifts my chin so he can look into my eyes. Two of the men have to hold Zee back as he struggles to get free. "A true mate is rare, my dear," he says. My skin is crawling with distaste. If I could, I'd rip his hand off my face.

I pull my head back away from his grip. "Get off me."

"Purple suits you. Is this what you came for?" He reaches for me again, but I manage to slip from his grasp.

"Leave her alone." Three men are now holding Zee in place. He twists and turns but doesn't break free.

"If only I could." The slimy alien touches me again. His dirty hands move over my arm. I try to step back, but he applies pressure to my bicep.

A helicopter starts to drown out the sounds from the ground, and the wind picks up. My hair blows wildly. "This is Corporal Janice Heeler from the United States Army. Put down your weapons and put your hands on your head," a loud voice says.

The aliens look at each other before Zee's uncle gives the signal. They open fire on the helicopter. Zee grabs a hold of me and lifts me over his shoulder. He carries me to the far side of the container out of the firing line. We can't see what's happening as he covers me with his huge body. The shots eventually stop and the helicopter lowers to the ground.

"Do you think it's safe for us to come out?"

"Wait here." He tries to move away, but I grip him tighter.

"No. You said we'd stay together."

He nods. "Okay."

We both put our hands on our heads and slowly leave our hiding place. Zee's uncle is lying face down on the floor, along with a couple of his men. The remaining two guys have surrendered.

"Prince Zenith and Naomi, I presume," Corporal

Heeler says. I know it's her because her voice is distinctive.

"Did my dad send you?" I ask. "Is everyone okay?"

"Don't worry, Miss. The situation is now under control."

I'm flooded with relief. I fling my arms around Zee, forgetting we're supposed to be showing we mean no harm. He picks me up, pulling me in for a kiss.

"Prince Zenith, you cannot leave us here," one of the aliens says as he carries me towards the helicopter.

"You threatened my mate. The army can do whatever they see fit with you now." His tone is dismissive.

We climb into the helicopter and the world seems to fade away as I nestle into Zee. He's alive, my dad is safe, and the danger has been neutralized. I could not be happier. The chopper takes off into the sky and we're finally going to get things back on track.

Wait. My future was mapped out. Sadness washes over me. I don't want Zee to leave, but he's a prince. He has responsibilities to his home planet.

There are a few things I need clarity on, though. His uncle suggested he came to Earth for a mate, and I need to know what it means. "Can I ask you a question?"

"Anything." He opens his arms, inviting me in.

"Did you come to Earth for a mate?" Whenever anyone has asked why he came to our planet, he's always made it sound like it was to save us. Could there be more to the story than that?

"I came to Earth for you." His answer is simple. Warmth fills me. He has a way with words that triggers something deep within. A feeling of love. Yet how can this work between us? We live lightyears apart. He's a leader; he needs to go home.

"What about the meteorite?"

"My destination was always to you. That was just something that stood in my way."

He kisses me, and at first, I hesitate as my mind runs into overdrive. He seems sincere about his feelings towards me, but what did he think would happen? Am I supposed to up and leave my life here on Earth? What about my new job? Could I really be happy on an alien planet?

CHAPTER TEN

Zee

Naomi is quiet for the rest of the journey. I have to trust the mating bond will settle whatever my words have unbalanced. She should know I care about her even if I wasn't honest about what I wanted from the start. I didn't want to scare her by coming on too strong.

Once we're reunited with her dad, she leaves me to talk to my men. The ship is now on land and the team is making progress in fixing it. The atmosphere is full of joy. Our mission is close to being a success and we're safe. We have everything to celebrate.

"Good to see you, Prince Zenith," Captain Jinker

says with a smile.

"Well done for thinking so fast when you were under attack." I clap to show I'm impressed.

"We did what we had to."

"You did an excellent job."

"We couldn't have done it without the help of the humans."

"They are quite spectacular," I say, looking over to where Naomi stands with her dad.

"I see you've found your mate. Congratulations."

"Thanks." Usually, I'd sit back and relax while my men worked, but something has changed since coming to Earth. I want to help, even if I'm not a mechanic or an engineer. I grab a sponge and help clean off the debris and seaweed from the exterior of the ship.

"We're going to celebrate tonight with a feast," Grayson announces, and Corporal Heeler agrees. There's a cheer from humans and aliens alike.

We finish up for the night before joining the banquet. The strange food tastes good, and I make sure I stay at Naomi's side.

"I'm so happy," she says, raising her glass to me.

"Everything worked out. Once our ship is fixed in the next day or two, all faith will be restored."

"And now I'm sad." She lowers the glass.

I frown. "Why? You should be happy. Everyone is safe and there's nothing that can't be repaired."

"But you'll be leaving."

"About that. I want you to come with me." This is the moment of truth. Is our bond cemented? Will she follow me to the ends of the solar system?

"I can't just drop everything and move to another planet."

"Why not?"

"I have a home, a job, and a family."

"I can give you all those things in Kamath."

"But they'll be yours, not mine."

"I don't understand. We're mates. We belong together."

"I'm human and you're an alien. We are from two different walks of life."

"I turned purple for you. You're mine. If you don't want to leave Earth, then we will stay." I nod. I'd already thought about this possible outcome.

"You would do that for me?"

"Have I not made myself clear?"

"What will you do here? Aren't you supposed to lead your people?"

"Deep down, none of these things matter. We can work it out. As I told you, you are mine and I'm yours. I will go where you go."

Her head wrinkles in worry, which isn't the reaction I wanted. "Tonight, I want you to come sleep at my apartment."

"Why? Are you unhappy?" Her facial expression has me questioning what she really wants. I have no problem sleeping in her nest, but I would've thought that would make her happy, not frown.

"I'm not unhappy. I like you, but reality will shake things up."

A true mate isn't something you choose. It's already written. She might think this is going to be hard, but I know it's going to work, even if we have a few hiccups. "I'm going to rock your world."

She laughs before a pink blush creeps up her face. "You already have."

I lean in and kiss her.

"Break it up," her dad says while a few of the humans and aliens cheer.

Naomi kisses me one last time before pulling away. "Sorry, Dad." A few of his friends laugh, which I don't understand, but I'm guessing it's a culture difference.

After the meal, we say our goodbyes. Her father is staying in a hotel with his friends. My men are staying at the ship. Naomi and I grab a cab so we can go to her apartment. I carry her up to her floor and she unlocks the door.

"It looks like my roommate's not home."

"I'm glad to get you all to myself."

We kiss, and she leads me into the bedroom.

***

I'm awake before Naomi, and I want to show her I can care for her. Hopefully, breakfast will be easy for me to make. I fill the coffee machine with water and change the filter. Once I've got that under control, I locate a pan with the ingredients to create a fried breakfast.

The food is almost ready when someone starts moving in the house. I haven't seen this person before, so it must be the roommate. "Greetings," I say.

"Hello." Her eyes are wide as she takes all of me in. "Naomi? Are you here, Naomi?" Her voice comes out unevenly like she's panicked.

I hold my hands up. Naomi told me about her roommate, and this must be her. "Don't scream. I'm not scary. I'm friendly, I promise. Sonya, is it?"

She moves her head from side to side. "You must be the alien Naomi mentioned she was giving a city tour. Prince Zenith?"

"Yes. That's me." I lower my arms as the fear leaves her face.

"It's nice to finally meet you." She holds out her hand and I shake it. I've seen enough human television to know this is the correct gesture.

Naomi stumbles out of the bedroom, rubbing her head. "Morning."

Sonya smirks. "It looks like you've had a good

night."

Naomi blushes. "Zee will be staying with us for a while. Is that okay?"

"Sure. I'm not going to complain about a half-naked man cooking in the kitchen."

I split the breakfast into three and we sit together.

"Have you heard from the school yet?" Sonya asks.

"Not yet. This is great, Zee. Thank you," Naomi says.

"It really is. Thanks, Zee." She salutes me before turning to Naomi. "When do you think you'll start?"

"The new term, as long as my paperwork comes back in time." Naomi pushes the food around her plate. My mate's still worried about how I fit here.

"And what about you? When are you leaving?" Sonya asks, and they both look at me.

"Apparently, he's staying." Naomi's eyes hold a question in which I need to reinforce faith. I'm not going anywhere without her unless she wishes it.

"Wow. Okay. What will you do in New York?"

Both of the women home in on me. Am I supposed to have all the answers right now? *No.* That would be impossible. "I have time to figure it out."

"What goals did you have back home?" Sonya seems to understand there's tension between us, but my answer won't ease her mind.

"I was going to be king."

Sonya's jaw drops and Naomi cringes.

"Can you really do this to him?" Sonya asks. Naomi has a strong bond with her people, and they sometimes forget I'm here, unless this is a human thing. She hasn't done anything to me. This is my choice.

Naomi's face drops. She runs her hands through her hair. "You know I'm a realist, but how else can I date someone with so much distance between us? Another planet is farther than anyone can manage."

"Do you think maybe you shouldn't be together?"

"No," we both say in unison. Our connection is real, and I'm glad Naomi can see it too.

After we finish breakfast, the girls go to get dressed.

"I think we should take you shopping for a shirt," Naomi says.

Looking down at my chest, I shrug. "What's wrong with my body?"

"Even my roommate can't keep her eyes off you."

"Are you jealous?" I frown.

"No. You're going to get a lot of attention, though, and I'd rather women had less of you to drool over."

I pull her into a hug. "You have nothing to worry about. I'm yours. Nobody else will have my affection, but I'll wear a shirt if you want me to."

We head out into the city. People stare at me in the street. I hold Naomi's hand tightly, ignoring the other humans. I want her to know I only have eyes for her. She picks out some clothes and shows me around some of the historical stores. Earth is completely different from Kamath. We live amongst nature rather than building up the land. Instead of concentrating on the differences, I focus on my woman. I'm determined to make this work.

CHAPTER ELEVEN

Naomi

Zee is trying to fit into my life and it's adorable. He's putting more effort in than any guy I've ever dated. He carries the groceries up to my apartment. Having a guy around when you don't have an elevator and live in an up-walk apartment is definitely a good idea.

Sonya has been giving us some space since she tried to open my eyes to the possibility our relationship could be a mistake. I see her point, but I'm blind to reason when it comes to Zee.

We snuggle on the couch. "Tell me something about you that nobody knows," Zee says.

I smile. "Like what?"

"Anything."

"Okay. If I do this, you have to do the same."

"Sure."

"Let me think." I touch my chin, trying to come up with something interesting. "When I was twelve, I used to pretend I could talk to animals. I'd convinced myself the fish at the local dentist wanted to be set free from their tank."

"To go in the ocean?"

"Precisely. Anyway, I made this plan to wait until the practice closed for the night, then I was going to break in."

"What happened?"

"When I arrived at the dental practice, the door was ajar. It turns out a robber had beaten me to the fish. He'd turned the place over looking for cash and even broke the tank. I saved the fish that day, but instead of putting them in the ocean, I put them in the sink. The moral of the story is they weren't saltwater fish and would've died if I'd gone through with my plan. I was a heroine that day. My reward was seeing the error of my ways."

"Are we only talking about fish?" Zee frowns, and his eyes hold a sadness I don't want to see.

I rub my hand through my hair and an ache starts in my chest. "I don't want to give you up. That doesn't mean this place is right for you. Do you think you'll be truly happy here?"

"All I need is you." He's so confident.

"Take me out of the equation. Is there any other reason you'd stay on Earth?" I need him to see I'm trying to be kind, even though it hurts.

"No."

My heart tells me to be selfish and reckless. My head is telling me I should try to see what's best for Zee. "I care for you, but I think you should leave with your ship."

Give me a better reason to make you stay.

"Why are you saying that?" Despair is written all over his face.

"We've only known each other a short time. Love shouldn't be this hard." My eyes start to water, and I fight back tears.

"That isn't what I want." He shakes his head.

I have to be strong. If he stays and resents me, it will be so much harder. "It's for the best." I put on a brave smile, even though there's nothing to be happy about.

He abruptly stands. "I need to leave."

He hugs me goodbye, and as quickly as he came into my life, he walks out.

I watch him go down the stairs. My heart is desperate to tell him to come back. Instead, I bite my tongue and let him go.

Once I'm alone, the tears start to fall. I really liked Zee. Maybe even love him. He's a great guy. This is the hardest decision I've ever made.

***

I take a shower before returning to the couch with a tub of chocolate ice cream. The contemporary romance I was reading no longer sounds appealing, so I watch a murder mystery while cuddling up with a fluffy blanket.

I'm three killers in when a low buzzing sound starts. At first, I try to ignore it, but it doesn't stop. I look around until I locate the source. Zee's alien tech has an incoming call.

"Hello," I say after pressing what I think is the right button. Has Zee called to say he can't live without me, or has he come up with a plan?

"Prince Zenith?" Captain Jinker says.

My heart sinks.

"Sorry, it's Naomi." My voice is deflated, just like my mood.

"Where is the prince?"

"He left over an hour ago." I frown. He should surely be back at his ship now.

"When will he be back?"

"He should be on his way to you, not me. Actually, he should be there." I switch the TV over to the news to see if something has happened, but it seems the aliens are yesterday's story.

"Why would he be on his way to the ship?"

"We decided to break things off and I thought he was going to return home with you." My bottom lip wobbles as tears threaten to fall from my eyes.

"He was leaving his mate behind?" He sounds outraged, like the idea isn't possible.

"Can you explain something to me? The way you and he reacted made it sound like it was life or death. What makes a mate so special? Surely he could find someone else." I was joking about the extreme circumstances, although it doesn't sound funny as it comes out. My heart aches for him.

"If an alien is rejected by his mate, he will not die, but there will be consequences. The pigment in his skin will fade and he will be forever grey to express his shame. Zee will not want or be able to take a new mate. He will be an outcast."

My breath hitches. "Why didn't he tell me this?"

"I do not know."

"We have to find him."

"Absolutely. I'll try and track the cruiser."

"I'll make my way down to the mothership."

"Excellent plan."

We hang up. I have to help Zee. If he wants to be with me over everything else, who am I to deny him? He *did* want to be with me more than anything. I'm such an idiot. Instead of pushing him away, I should have asked him what I could do to help him.

I put my boots on and leave my apartment. I have to find Zee so we can work this out. Instead of heading for the underground, I flag down a cab.

"Where to?" he asks once I'm inside.

I'm about to give the location of the ship when it dawns on me. Where's the one place he would go? When we first met, I took him to the aquarium. Would he go there to relax and escape? "Take me to the bus station."

He does as I ask. While we're making our way across the city, I check my news app. Unfortunately, I come up empty. From the bus station, I make my way to the aquarium. The location I think Zee is at isn't close, so I hope I'm right.

A tingle spreads over my skin. Zee is here. I can feel it. The large tank with the sharks is where I find him on a bench. I sit down next to him.

"Hi."

He turns his head. "Hello."

"What are you doing here?"

"Thinking." He rubs his hand over his face.

"Care to share?"

"When I left Kamath, I thought I'd find my mate. She'd swoon at my feet, and we would return home together ready to start a family. I've messed everything up."

I put my arms around him. "You have not. I love you. That has to count for something." As soon as the words are out, I know they're true. My feelings will not waver, and time won't change that. We're true mates. Our bond is forever.

"Fate brought us together. I know how you feel about me because you're my true mate. We are made for each other." He leans in and kisses me. It's filled with passion. It's perfect.

Zee is everything I didn't realize I needed. I'm done fighting the bond. We have to make this work, even if it means leaving my home. Maybe Kamath is my destiny.

CHAPTER TWELVE

Zee

"Are you sure about this?" I ask.

"Yes. This feels right," Naomi says, kissing my cheek. We talked through our options and came to a solution that suited all. I could not be happier to be going home with my girl.

"You have time for kissing later. Move off the loading bay," Ralph says.

"Yes sir," I say, pulling my mate into my arms so I can carry her to a safer make-out spot.

"Are you sure you need another fish tank, Dad?" Naomi asks.

"If my friends and I are going to study the marine life on Kamath, we're going to need everything we have here." He gestures to the diving gear and multiple containers. Naomi assures me he's enthusiastic about moving to my planet. He waves us off as he drags another box onto the ship. "Go back to kissing. You don't need to know how much equipment we're bringing."

"Ignore him," Martin says, placing two suitcases onto the cargo bay.

Naomi rolls her eyes.

"Maybe we should leave them to it," I say, pulling her farther onto the ship. Once we'd had time to talk about how our relationship would work, everything fell into place. In Kamath, her dad will be close by, and she'll be able to teach the males interested in finding a human mate.

My dad will be pleased with my work and I'm sure he'll love Naomi.

I take her to our private quarters and close the door to the rest of the world. "Welcome to our tranquil space." I throw her down on the bed.

"Don't you need to oversee the ship's take-off?" Naomi asks.

I kiss up her neck, ready to forget about everyone else. "I'm sure Captain Jinker and your dad will have it under control." All of the men have been displaying an overload of testosterone.

I'm looking forward to being on home ground where we'll return to our usual roles. Even Naomi's dad will be where he loves with the sea life, and dominance will be restored between the men.

She giggles as I blow raspberries on her belly. "You can't shrug off your responsibilities."

I lift her top a little more, peppering kisses all over her until I reach her lips. Once I'm towering over her, I suck on her bottom lip, holding on to the fantasy it's just the two of us for a bit longer. "Just let me have a few more minutes of bliss. I'm going to enjoy having you in this room while we travel."

"Me too. This still feels like a dream."

"I'm going to fulfill your fantasies every day."

She smiles. "I like that idea." We kiss again.

Taking her hand, I pull her to her feet. "Let's get this ship off the ground so we can get back to enjoying each other."

"Yes, sir." She winks, and it's so tempting to throw

her back on the bed. Instead, we make our way to the control room.

"Have the final checks been carried out?" Captain Jinker asks.

Hix presses a few buttons. "We are ready to go."

I look around. The humans and aliens look ready for me to give the order. "Let's get out of here."

Everyone cheers. Jinker commands his team, and we lift off. Everyone cheers as the underneath us begins to fade away. I hug Naomi, and she smiles widely. This is the beginning of everything else, and I'm excited to find out what that means.

The End

Acknowledgement

With every book I write, there's always a team that helps me perfect the final version. I'd like to thank Karen, Tori, Rebecca, Melanie, and Jackie. You are my conscience, confidence, and cheerleaders. Lastly, I'd like to thank everyone who believes in me. Enjoy the rides I create. You never know what I'll bring you next ;).

About The Author

Danielle lives in Yorkshire, England, with her husband, daughter, and tortoise. She enjoys reading, watching the rain, and listening to old music. Her dreams include writing stories, visiting magical places, and staying young at heart. The people who know her describe her as someone who has her head in the clouds and her mind in a book.

OTHER BOOKS BY DANIELLE JACKS

Kickflip Summer
The Heart of Baker Bay
Dirty Kisses and Conflicting Wishes
Burned by Fire
Confessions of a Sophomore Prankster
Romance Under Aquarius
Twisted Bond
I Dare You
Faking it with Archie
Birthday Boy

Printed in Great Britain
by Amazon